Dear Parents,

Welcome to the Scholastic Reader series. We have taken over 80 years of experience with teachers, parents, and children and put it into a program that is designed to match your child's interests and skills.

Level 1—Short sentences and stories made up of words kids can sound out using their phonics skills and words that are important to remember.

Level 2—Longer sentences and stories with words kids need to know and new "big" words that they will want to know.

Level 3—From sentences to paragraphs to longer stories, these books have large "chunks" of texts and are made up of a rich vocabulary.

Level 4—First chapter books with more words and fewer pictures.

It is important that children learn to read well enough to succeed in school and beyond. Here are ideas for reading this book with your child:

• Look at the book together. Encourage your child to read the title and make a prediction about the story.
• Read the book together. Encourage your child to sound out words when appropriate. When your child struggles, you can help by providing the word.
• Encourage your child to retell the story. This is a great way to check for comprehension.
• Have your child take the fluency test on the last page to check progress.

Scholastic Readers are designed to support your child's efforts to learn how to read at every age and every stage. Enjoy helping your child learn to read and love to read.

> **—Francie Alexander**
> Chief Education Officer
> Scholastic Education

To Lia
— G.M.

To Isaak, Wes, Leo, and Arlo
— B.L.

The author gratefully acknowledges Jordan Riesman
for his contribution to this book.

Text copyright © 2003 by Grace Maccarone.
Illustrations copyright © 2003 by Betsy Lewin.
Activities copyright © 2005 Scholastic Inc.
All rights reserved. Published by Scholastic Inc.
SCHOLASTIC, CARTWHEEL BOOKS, FIRST-GRADE FRIENDS, and associated logos
are trademarks and/or registered trademarks of Scholastic Inc.

Library of Congress Cataloging-in-Publication Data is available.

ISBN: 0-439-38575-X

10 9 8 7 6 5 4 3   08 09
Printed in the U.S.A. 23 • First printing, February 2003

THE SLEEP OVER

by **Grace Maccarone**

Illustrated by **Betsy Lewin**

Scholastic Reader — Level 1

SCHOLASTIC INC. Cartwheel ·B·O·O·K·S· ®

New York Toronto London Auckland Sydney
Mexico City New Delhi Hong Kong Buenos Aires

Sam packs PJ's,
underwear.
Sam does not pack
Huggy Bear.

Sam packs a comb,
fresh clothes to wear,
a toothbrush . . .

and his Huggy Bear.

Sam gets inside
the SUV.

"Tonight I'll sleep at Dan's. Yippee!"

"Come here," says Mom.
"Let me kiss you.
Have fun tonight.
I will miss you!"

"Come in," Dan says.
"I'm glad you came.
Max is here.
Let's play a game."

They play a game,
then play another.

"It's time to eat, boys," calls Dan's mother.

Sam is hungry,
so Sam eats a
salad and a slice
of pizza.

They brush their teeth

and wash their faces,

put on pajamas . . .

and pick their places.

"Let's watch a movie on TV,"
Dan says.
The other boys agree.

At ten o'clock,
the movie ends.
It's sleepy time
for three good friends.

Dan's mom comes in
to close the light.
She says, "Good night.
Sweet dreams. Sleep tight."

But Sam needs Huggy.

He goes to get her.

Now Sam has Huggy,
and Sam feels better.

But Sam can't sleep.
He misses his mother.
He misses his dad.
He misses his brother.

He tells Dan's mom.

She tells Sam's dad.

Now Dad is here,
and Sam is glad.

So Sam goes home.

He gets there fast.

And Sam is in
his bed —
at last!

When morning comes,
Sam's on his way
to Dan's where he'll
eat eggs and play.

The three boys
have a happy day!